For Pat and Sheila

THE TIME IT TOOK TOM

Nick Sharratt
Stephen Tucker

LITTLE TIGER PRESS

With thanks to
David Fickling, Ness Wood
and John Peacock

LITTLE TIGER PRESS
N16 W23390 Stoneridge Drive, Waukesha, WI 53188
First published in United States 1999
First published in Great Britain 1998 by
Scholastic Children's Books, London
a division of Scholastic Ltd
Text copyright © Nick Sharratt and Stephen Tucker, 1998
Illustration copyright © Nick Sharratt, 1998
CIP Data is available
ISBN 1-888444-63-0
Printed in China
First American edition
1 3 5 7 9 10 8 6 4 2

Tom found the red paint.

It took him three seconds
to decide what to
do with it.

One.

Two.

Three.

It took him (*oof!*) three (*humpf!*) minutes to get the (*grrrrrrrrrrrrr!*) lid off the can!

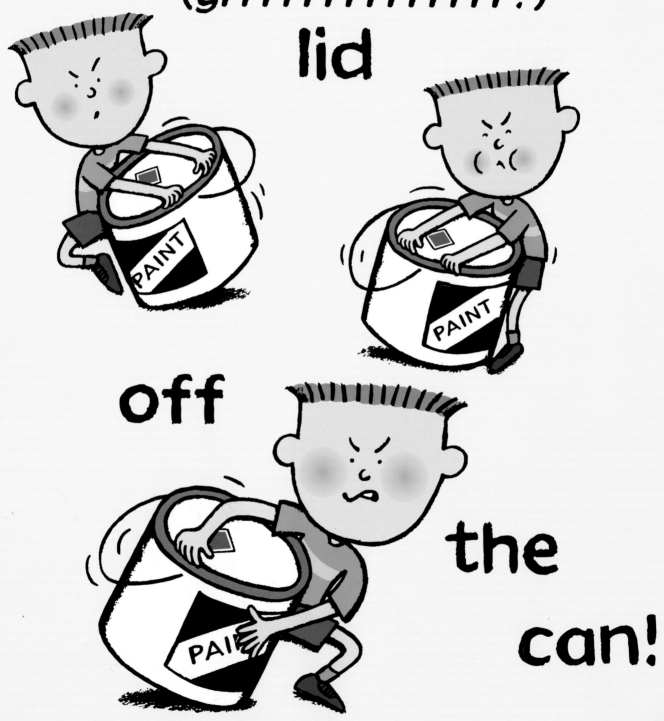

It took him three hours to paint the living room.

One hour.

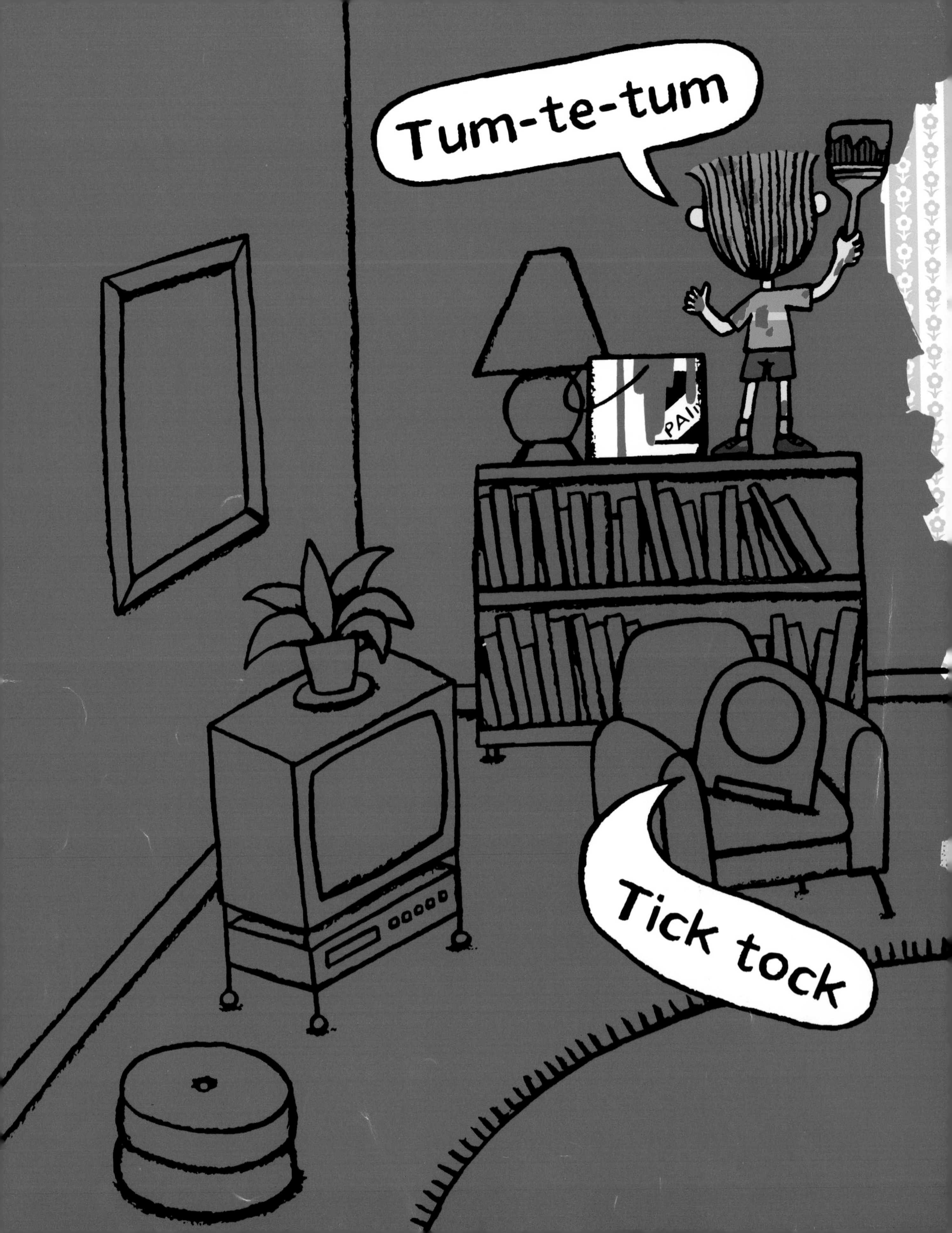
Tum-te-tum
Tick tock

Tom's mom came in.
It took her *ten*

nine

eight

seven

six

five

four

three

two

one

seconds to **explode!**

It took three weeks.

And this is how we did it.

"We had to get a dumpster
For the ruined pieces of furniture.

We stripped off all the wallpaper,
And went off to the store

To buy some cans of paint
(There were lots of different colors),
And pick a paper that we liked
From all the ones we saw.

We sandpapered the woodwork
And we painted it with primer.
We started putting gloss paint
On the window frame and door.

And that's when Mom decided

 That she didn't like the color,

So we stopped what we were doing

And we went back to the store.

Here's a list of what we painted:

The window  and the baseboard,

The bookcase and the table

And the sideboard  and the door.

 And this time Mom was happy,

And I was even happier

Because I really didn't feel

 Like painting anymore!

 Mom hung the paper (by herself!)

Men came and laid the carpet

And after that we had to make

A last trip to the store . . .

For a couch 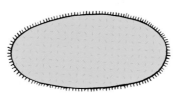 and an armchair

 And a **TV** and a **VCR**,

Some curtains for the window,

And a new rug
for the floor.

We also bought a little tree

(But that was for the yard)

And a footstool and a fruit bowl

And a nice plant in a pot,

Cushions,   lamps, a mirror,

Some pictures of the countryside,

A clock, a vase,

A picture frame,

And that was it!

One year went by.

Two years

went by.

Three   years went by.

Tom found the blue paint.

E

Sharratt, Nick.
    The time it
took Tom

p1495   3/00